Little
Peter's Railway
The Picnic

by
Christopher Vine

The watercolour illustrations are by John Wardle

Published by
Christopher Vine 2012

Printed by The Amadeus Press
Copyright © 2012 Christopher Vine

ISBN 978-1-9088970-22

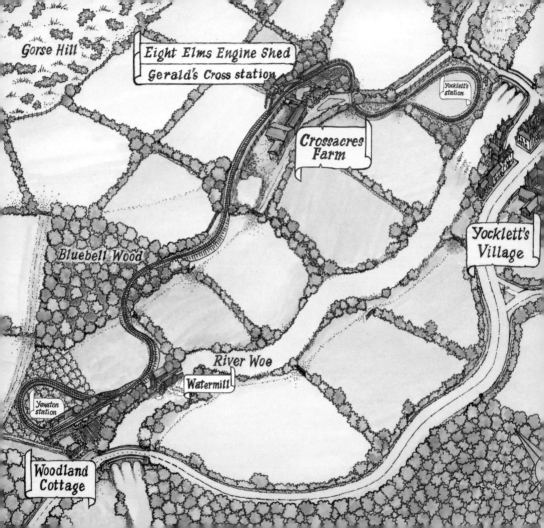

The Peter's Railway Series

The railway built by Peter and his Grandpa runs across the farm, between their houses. It makes visiting each other a lot of fun and there have been many adventures along the line.

The locomotive, Fiery Fox, belongs to Mr Esmond, but Peter and Grandpa have made everything else themselves: The track, wagons and even the little buildings at the stations.

In this story Grandpa is left looking after the family. Whatever will he do to entertain Peter and the young twins, Kitty and Harry? And what will it lead to?

The Picnic

Grandpa was driving the small steam train down the line to Woodland Cottage. Grandma was riding in her special saloon carriage.

She was going to the cinema later with Peter's Mum and Dad. Peter and the twins, Kitty and Harry, were staying at home with Grandpa.

Grandma and Mum gave him lots of instructions. "There's a beef stew, don't forget to heat it up..." "Make sure they are all in bed by seven o'clock..." "Get them to brush their teeth..."

They were still giving poor Grandpa his orders as they drove off down the road.

Grandpa however, had his own ideas on how to entertain children!

When they had gone, he went into the kitchen to start cooking dinner. Through the window he could see the children, out on the railway. Peter was filling the tender of Fiery Fox with water, while Harry was pushing Kitty along the line in a coal wagon.

Grandpa didn't know much about cooking, but heating up the beef stew was easy enough. He could put jacket potatoes in the oven at the same time, but what else would go with it?

'I know,' he thought to himself. 'I'll boil up some cabbage and Brussels sprouts. That will make a really healthy meal.'

It never occurred to him that the children might not like cabbage and sprouts.

"Dinner time," he called out of the window. "And I've got an easy question for you.

"Would you like to eat in the boring old kitchen?" he asked them. "Or would it be more fun to go for a picnic on the train?"

"Picnic, Picnic, Picnic!" everyone shouted. So they carried all the food and drink outside and loaded it onto the wagons.

"Can we have the picnic by the river, at the waterfall?" asked Peter.

"Of course we can," replied Grandpa laughing. "Jump on quickly and let's go while the food's still hot."

"I'll drive the train," he continued, "then you can all enjoy the ride and think about how hungry you are!"

When they were all aboard, Grandpa climbed onto the locomotive and checked the boiler. The water level was fine and the fire was burning bright and hot. He gave a toot on the whistle and cracked open the steam regulator.

With a few wheezes and chuffs, Fiery Fox eased slowly out of the little station. Clouds of white steam pouring out of her chimney.

It was a pretty run on the railway, with the first part of the line running through the orchard behind the house. After that the railway entered a field and ran along beside the River Woe.

"Faster Grandpa, Faster!" shouted the twins.

Grandpa opened the regulator further and Fiery Fox raced across the field. The children laughed as their hair blew back in the wind.

Now they could see the waterfall in the distance and Grandpa started to slow down. He stopped right beside the watermill which they had built last summer.

It was turning quietly, generating electricity to power the house and farm. With the water rushing over the rocks and dry grass to sit on, it was the perfect place for a picnic.

The sun was low in the sky and they tucked into the food like hungry lions.

They all started with a plate stacked high with beef stew, baked potatoes, cabbage and Brussels sprouts.

It was so much fun eating outside that Peter and the twins completely forgot that they didn't like cabbage and sprouts. They just ate everything.

"More cabbage please Grandpa," shouted Harry.

"More sprouts please Grandpa," shouted Kitty.

"More of everything," sang out Peter.

Grandpa piled their plates up again and the party fell silent while they demolished every last scrap of food.

When they were finished, Grandpa told them about steam engine drivers in the old days.

"If the train was stopped for a long time at a red signal," he began, "the driver and fireman could cook up a really good breakfast in the cab.

"They would heat the coal shovel by holding it in the flames in the firebox," he explained. "Then they would take it out, wipe it clean and add some cooking fat and sausages, or bacon and eggs.

"Then they held the shovel back in the firebox until it was cooked to perfection.

"I've got some mini sausages here," he chuckled. "Let's cook them in Fiery Fox!"

Apart from the one which fell into the fire, they were the best sausages they had ever tasted.

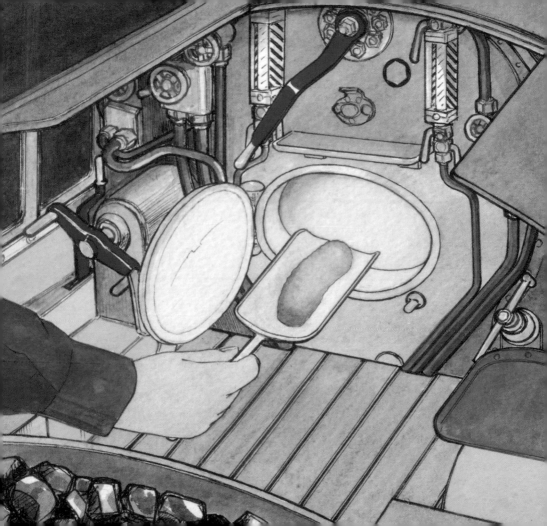

It was nearly time to drive the engine back home, but Grandpa had some work to do first.

"We'll go round the line to Bluebell Wood," he explained. "I've cut some logs for your dad. We can load them onto the train and take them back to Woodland Cottage to burn on the fire."

By the time they stopped it was after nine o'clock and almost dark. "Oh dear," muttered Grandpa. "Quick everyone, run inside and jump into bed.

"Don't worry about changing into your pyjamas, just be in bed before Mum gets home. If she finds you still up and about, I shall be in big trouble. Again!" he added.

Next day, late in the afternoon, the children were upstairs in Peter's room, playing trains. Mum was downstairs, cooking dinner for her young family.

Tonight it was sausages again, their favourite. And cabbage and sprouts, not so favourite. Or so she thought.

"Dinner's ready," she called. But just then, the doorbell rang and she went to see who it was. When she came back there was no sign of the children, but the food had disappeared.

All was quiet in the house until a peculiar noise started coming down through the ceiling. A whirring, rumbling and giggling sort of noise.

Mum went up to investigate..........

Very quietly she opened the door a little and peeked inside. Nobody noticed so she just watched.

A sausage was going round on a small wagon on the model railway. Then a sprout whizzed past!

"Another sausage please Peter," called Harry, as he drove his engine and empty trucks round the line to his brother.

Peter, who had all the plates, put a sausage on the little train and Harry drove it back and ate it quickly, laughing.

Kitty's train was on the inner circuit and it was loaded up with a full meal. She was driving it round and round, picking things off to eat as it went past. Very tricky with the cabbage.

"I'm thirsty," shouted Harry above the din. "Could you send over the milk train Peter?"

Mum could hardly believe her eyes as a small shunting locomotive pulled a long tanker wagon out of a siding. It clanked round the line and stopped in front of the three children.

"Opening the milk tanks!" announced Peter, as he pulled off their tiny lids.

"Drink up!" shouted Kitty and they each put a straw into the hole in the top. A few seconds later there were funny sucking noises and it was all gone.

"Cabbage please this time," called Harry.

"More sprouts please," yelled Kitty.

Peter loaded them up and off they went.

Poor Mum. She had always struggled to get them to eat healthy vegetables and now they were wolfing them down like there was no tomorrow.

Then suddenly - Disaster! While no one was looking, Harry switched some points and diverted his train onto Kitty's line.

Smash! The two trains collided head on and food went everywhere. One engine got buried in cabbage and the other got stuck on a sausage!

Oh dear, what a mess. This was going to take a lot of clearing up.

Mum sighed quietly and shut the door. Whatever would they get up to next...?

The End.

Why Peter's Railway?

Since a very small boy, Chris has always loved everything mechanical, especially steam engines. The first workshop was in his bedroom where he made an electric go-kart aged 8, followed by a mini-bike powered by the engine from a petrol lawn mower.

He spent many holidays on a friend's farm where there was a miniature railway across a field and so started a love of making model steam locomotives. The latest is Bongo, 8 feet long and the inspiration for Fiery Fox in the books.

Chris wanted to share his love and knowledge of railways and engineering: Peter's Railway is the result.

Story   **Technical**   **Adventure**

The original books

The original four books tell the charming story of Peter and his Grandpa building and running their steam railway across the farm. At the ends of chapters are special how-it-works pages with simple (but accurate) explanations of what has been happening in the story. In addition, Grandpa tells some wonderful stories from the old days on the railways. Age range 6 - 12 years approx.

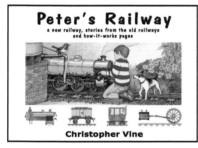

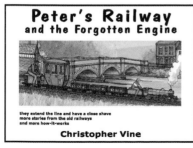

Hardback, 96 pages 17 x 24 cm with 30 watercolour pictures by John Wardle and 14 pages of clearly explained technical drawings. £11.99

Paperback books

A series of Peter's Railway in a smaller format. While the original books each contain several story or adventure threads, separate technical pages and Grandpa's tales, the small books concentrate on one aspect; an adventure, a tale from the old railways or a technical book.

"Little" Peter's Railway are gentle stories for younger children.

Peter saves Christmas.

A bed-time story with a twist...

Grandpa answers a tricky question.

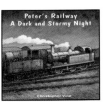
A dramatic true story from the old days.

Grandpa entertains the children and mayhem follows...

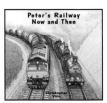
A cab-ride in a modern train and a tale of a near disaster.

Our two heroes make a new engine.

A true story about an unlucky locomotive.